VELVET

THE SECRET LIVES OF DEAD MEN

ED BRUBAKER
WRITER

STEVE EPTING
ARTIST

ELIZABETH BREITWEISER
COLORS

CHRIS ELIOPOULOS
LETTERS

ERIC STEPHENSON
EDITS

DREW GILL
PRODUCTION

SPECIAL THANKS TO SIDNEY STONE

A NOTE ON FOREIGN LANGUAGES:
Dialogue in an italic font should be read as a foreign language.

VELVET, VOLUME 2: THE SECRET LIVES OF DEAD MEN. First printing. May 2015. ISBN: 978-1-63215-234-3.

PRAGUE - 1956

THIS IS MR. *THACKERAY*...I THINK WE TOOK A *WRONG TURN.*

CAN YOU GIVE ME *NEW DIRECTIONS,* PLEASE?

I THOUGHT THE MISSION--
THE *MISSION* WAS FINE...

"EVERYTHING WENT JUST AS PLANNED. NO ALARMS RAISED.

"BUT THEN AT THE SAFE HOUSE, GUSTAV SAID SOMETHING... SOME JOKE...
"...ABOUT AGENT MOCKINGBIRD.

"HOW THE HELL HE KNEW ABOUT THAT, I'D LIKE TO KNOW...

"BUT WE WON'T BE FINDING OUT.
"I HAD TO DRAG HER OFF OF HIM."

CHRIST.
I TOLD YOU, SIR...

...I TOLD YOU SHE WAS IN NO SHAPE TO GO BACK INTO THE FIELD.

THE SECRET LIVES OF DEAD MEN

Part One

LONDON – 1973

I'm too smart to return to England. They know that.

Which is why I breeze right through Heathrow.

Because they aren't looking for me there.

CUSTOM

But two or three days should be more than enough.

I wasn't planning to stay hidden that long anyway.

Because the answers I need are inside the agency...

...and there's no quiet way to get them.

London feels different.
RIGHT... THIS WAY THEN...

I've only been gone a month, but it's like I'm seeing it with different eyes...

Or maybe I'm just seeing what I've been pretending **not to** all these years.

YOU? IT'S BEEN HELL OF A LONG TIME, GIRLIE.
BUT YOU'VE STILL GOT WHAT I NEED, PEG?
'***COURSE*** I BLOODY DO.
WHO'D YOU THINK YOU'RE ***DEALING*** WITH?

--had I just while I was desk?
Because I didn't think of it that way at the time.
I'd come home from the Bahamas shattered.
I careened from suicidal to homicidal...
...on my way to a complete nervous breakdown.
That's what happens when you're ordered to kill your own husband on your honeymoon, it turns out.
You lose your mind.

So, back then, that desk was what saved me.

YOU'RE TOO VALUABLE TO THE *AGENCY*, TEMPLETON... YOUR EXPERIENCE IN THE FIELD, YOUR *MIND...*

YOU'D BE DOING *ME* THE FAVOR HERE...

But it wasn't temporary.
No, the years had flown by...because that's what they do.

And the whole time, the thing that had broken me was a lie.
Richard--Codename Mockingbird--had never been a mole.

Someone inside ARC-7 had played me...
Now they were playing me again, and turning the whole agency against me to do it.

So...who in the hell was I after?

There were only a few left from the early days who'd reached any **real position** of power...
So, assuming I was only looking for **one** man--and considering what had happened to **MI-6,** there was no **guarantee** of that--these were my likely suspects.
Lt. Director Simonson.
Simonson had always been a prick, but back then, he was still in the early days of his race up the ladder.
EYES ONLY
ALLIED RECONNAISSANCE COMMISSION
I have to wonder if a double-agent would be so **obviously** ambitious...
But Simonson **did** have knowledge of most of ARC-7s missions at the time...so I can't cross him off my list.

And Director Manning? No.
He was one of the few men I'd actually call noble, and he'd kept my secrets all these years.
I really don't want to believe it's him.

Jean Bellanger, who now ran our Paris Station...
...that was a man I could believe almost anything of.
There was something dead behind his eyes.

In 1956, he was one of Manning's closest advisors.
A cold calculating bastard was sometimes just who you needed.

And **Senator Hillerman**...who wasn't **officially** in the agency anymore.

But until his political career, he'd either **run** or been **second-in-command** of all our U.S. operations.

X-14 had several missions on American soil the past few years. It's possible he'd crossed Hillerman's path...

Stumbled onto something that had gotten him killed.

This is **another** problem with spies...it's too easy to imagine **any** of them being a **double**.

All they did was **lie** or **keep secrets**.

I had to widen my field of inquiry if I was going to solve this...
And to do that, I'd need to recruit an asset.
Luckily, I already had one in mind.
See, I didn't just come to Soho for its black market weapons trade.
AH, NO...NO. I MEANT THE OTHER...
...GIRL...
HELLO, ELODIE...
I'M AFRAID I TOLD THE OTHER GIRL TO TAKE THE REST OF THE NIGHT OFF.

VELVET...?
DON'T WORRY, I'M NOT HERE TO SHOOT YOU.

NO. OF COURSE YOU AREN'T...
WHAT THEY ARE SAYING ABOUT YOU, IT **CANNOT** BE TRUE.

SO...WHAT DO YOU **NEED?** WHAT CAN I DO?
*Recruiting assets isn't **usually** this easy.*

But ever since Elodie had transferred in from Paris, I'd noticed something odd...
*This **way** she looked at me when she thought I wasn't watching.*

*It was how I had looked at **Lady Pauline.** Like a fan.*

That's how I knew she'd read my files...which there was NO WAY she had security clearance to do.
...AND THEN IT'S ECHO ECHO NINE.
CHANGING ON TUESDAYS STILL?
YES.

But this girl, she was a sneaky little vixen. Clearly.
BUT THIS IS ALL THAT YOU WANT?
I COULD BE OF MUCH MORE USE TO YOU.

I'M NOT LOOKING FOR A SIDEKICK...
AND TRUST ME, YOU'RE FAR TOO OBVIOUS TO SEND ON COVERT MISSIONS INTO THE RECORDS ROOM.

I CAN BE COVERT.

HIDING THAT YOU'RE A LESBIAN INTO KINK ISN'T THE SAME AS COMMITTING HIGH TREASON...

...BUT I DO APPRECIATE THE SENTIMENT.
HOW ABOUT YOU JUST TELL ME HOW CLOSE TO MY TRAIL THEY ARE?

WELL, HE TOOK AN **ENTIRE TEAM** TO BELGRADE AFTER THE REPORT ABOUT THE GENERAL AND HIS WIFE.
THEY'RE DUE BACK TOMORROW, HAVING NOT **FOUND** YOU.

I TAKE HIS MESSAGES FOR THE LIEUTENANT...
HE LIKES TO SWEAR, THIS **SERGEANT ROBERTS.**
YEAH, I DIDN'T LIKE HIM MUCH EVEN **BEFORE** HE WAS HUNTING ME...

SO...HOW'S **MEGAN?**
HARD TO SAY...SHE'S BEEN **DISTANT** SINCE SHE TOOK OVER YOUR **DESK.**

I'M SURPRISED YOU DIDN'T GO TO **HER.** WEREN'T YOU TWO GOOD FRIENDS?

WE WERE BUT...THAT FEELS LIKE A LIFETIME AGO.

ANYWAY, THEY'RE PROBABLY **WATCHING** HER...

Except I know they're **not.**

I shadowed Megan from her flat to the tube station this morning, and there wasn't even a **hint** of surveillance.

They'll get word of my false passport being flagged by the end of day, maybe even by this afternoon.

So it's time, then.

But I have another problem.
I SAID--

Whoever set me up is watching the agency hunt me.
--UKTT--

Maybe even helping with the pursuit.

And I left a trail in Yugoslavia, like some amateur.

So pretty soon they're going to figure out that I'm not just running.
AHH--!
And then there won't be anything left to find.
Because this person knows how to cover their ass...
They do it with a shotgun to the face...
Or a lie to a trained killer.

So the only way I'm going to **solve** this...

Because like I said, the answers I need are **inside** the agency...

...and there's no **quiet way** to get them.

SORRY ABOUT YOUR *MEN*, DIRECTOR...

I DON'T THINK I HURT THEM *TOO* BADLY.

TEMPLETON...? WHAT'RE YOU *DOING?*

YOU NEED TO *COME IN* WITH ME, WE CAN SORT THIS... WE--

TURN MYSELF IN? NO. I DON'T *THINK* SO.

GET IN THE *CAR*, SIR...

I'LL DRIVE.

COLT

I DON'T CARE WHAT MY ORDERS ARE...
STOP!
...I THINK I'M GOING TO KILL HER.

THAT'S THE FOURTH TIME THIS MISSION'S LED ME RIGHT INTO ENEMY FIRE...

THIS IS WHY I HATE HUNTING SPIES.

GIVE ME POLITICIANS OR BORED SOCIALITES OR GOVERNMENT SCIENTISTS...
BUT SPIES ARE ALL TOTAL BASTARDS... EVEN THE FEMALE OF THE SPECIES.
HERE'S HOW A SPY DISAPPEARS...
THEY MAKE IT LOOK LIKE THEY WENT TO TEN DIFFERENT CITIES ALL OVER THE WORLD AT THE SAME TIME, THEN THEY GO SOMEWHERE ELSE.
AND MEN LIKE ME HAVE TO RUN DOWN EVERY ONE OF THOSE LEADS, JUST IN CASE.
IT'S ONE OF THE MAIN WEAPONS IN OUR FIELD...THE SMOKESCREEN.
MY FRIEND AT MI-6 CALLS IT "CHICKENFEED."
UKK--!

BITS OF INTEL LEAKED TO MAKE AN ENEMY THINK THEY'VE GOT SOMETHING GOLDEN.
OR TO MAKE THEM THINK EVERYTHING ELSE THEY'VE GOT IS SHIT.
IT'S A TECHNIQUE OUR MISS TEMPLETON KNOWS WELL...
WHICH IS WHY I STOPPED CHASING HER OBVIOUS TRAIL THREE DAYS AGO.
SO HOW THE HELL DID A KGB HIT SQUAD GET TO FRANKFURT BEFORE ME?
SHE CAN'T REALLY BE THAT GOOD, CAN SHE?

PART TWO

MY PROBLEM IS, ALL I EVER DID WAS UNDERESTIMATE HER... APPARENTLY.

SHE WAS JUST THE GIRL SITTING NEXT TO THE DIRECTOR, TAKING NOTES.

ANOTHER SECRETARY TO FLIRT WITH, IF A BIT HARDER TO CRACK THAN THE REST...

MOVE ALONG, X-33...DON'T YOU HAVE A PLANE TO CATCH?

THAT'D BE CLASSIFIED INFORMATION, TEMPLETON... EYES ONLY.

TAHITI... PSSH...
CALL ME WHEN THEY SEND YOU SOMEPLACE GOOD.

MAYBE I WILL, TEMPLETON...OR MAYBE I'LL BRING YOU ALONG.
SURE YOU WILL...

NOW GET OFF MY DESK, COLT...
ONE OF US HAS WORK TO DO.

BUT IT TURNS OUT SHE WAS QUITE A LOT MORE THAN THAT, ONCE UPON A TIME.
LOOKING AT HER FILE, I'M IMPRESSED AS HELL... AND I FEEL LIKE A FOOL.

HOW CAN I NOT HAVE SEEN EVEN A HINT OF WHAT SHE REALLY WAS?

OF COURSE, EVEN AFTER I KNOW THE TRUTH, I **STILL** UNDERESTIMATE HER...
SHE'S LONG OUT OF THE FIELD, SHE'S **GOT** TO BE RUSTY... OR SO I **FIGURE...**

SO I FIGURE **INCORRECTLY.**
I SPEND A WEEK RUNNING ALL OVER THE WORLD CHASING HER SMOKE...

THEN I GET MY FIRST REAL LEAD, WHO TURNS OUT TO BE AUSTRIA'S BIGGEST **CRIME LORD.**
AND HE'S IN NO MOOD FOR **TALKING,** UNLESS IT'S ABOUT HIS YACHT.
WHICH APPARENTLY SHE STOLE.

I'D EXPECT HER TO BE STAYING UNDER THE RADAR...
BUT SHE ISN'T... IN FACT, IT ALMOST SEEMS LIKE SHE'S FUCKING WITH ME.

THE DAY AFTER MY *INCIDENT* IN VIENNA, ONE OF HER FALSE TRAILS LEADS ME TO A *KGB FRONT* AT A FOREIGN NEWSPAPER OFFICE.

THESE MEN ARE *ALSO* NOT PLEASED TO SEE ME.

THAT'S WHEN I START TO THINK NONE OF THIS MAKES SENSE.
IF SHE'S A DOUBLE-AGENT, WHY LEAVE A TRAIL OF BREADCRUMBS TO AN *ENEMY* OUTPOST?

AND WHY RISK EXPOSING HERSELF IN YUGOSLAVIA JUST DAYS AFTER STIRRING UP TROUBLE IN VIENNA?

THIS WAS NOT THE BEHAVIOR OF A TRAINED SPY TRYING TO DISAPPEAR...

...EVEN SERGEANT ROBERTS HAD TO AGREE WITH THAT.
WE THINK WE KNOW WHY SHE WAS IN BELGRADE...
I MEAN, WE DON'T KNOW... BUT...

WHAT'S THE THEORY, THEN?

THAT SHE WAS TRACING ONE OF X-14'S RECENT MISSIONS.
EXCUSE ME?

I KNOW HOW IT SOUNDS...
BUT THE TWO DEAD BODIES SHE LEFT BEHIND WERE *BOTH* PART OF HIS MISSION.
SO SHE KILLS X-14 AND THEN STARTS BACKTRACKING HIS MOVEMENTS?
PANETTERIA Specialità BISCOTTI ALLA CASTAGNA

THIS IS *HORSESHIT*, ROBERTS...THINK ABOUT IT FOR *FIVE SECONDS...*
SHE'S NOT RUNNING. SHE'S INVESTIGATING.

OF COURSE *YOU'D* LOOK AT IT LIKE THAT.
YOU PEOPLE, FIELD OPS...THINK YOU'RE SO DIFFERENT...

DID IT NEVER *OCCUR* TO YOU SHE MIGHT BE CLEANING UP A *MESS?*
SHE KILLED THE MAN FOR A *REASON*, AFTER ALL...

MAYBE SHE WANTS TO MAKE SURE NO ONE *ELSE* FINDS WHATEVER X-14 DID.

AND YOU DON'T THINK SHE'D TRY TO BE A LITTLE LESS *PUBLIC* IF THAT WAS HER PLAN?
I WOULD HAVE *THOUGHT* SO, YES.
BUT WE'RE TALKING ABOUT A WOMAN WHO KNOWS *ALL* OUR PROCEDURES AND PROTOCOLS...

SHE KNOWS HOW WE'LL RESPOND TO JUST ABOUT *ANY* MOVE SHE MAKES.

MAYBE THE EXACT THING SHE WANTS IS *US* HERE IN THIS BAR, ARGUING ABOUT WHETHER SHE'S GUILTY...

SO I'LL JUST GO BY THE *EVIDENCE...*
...AND VELVET TEMPLETON HAS LEFT A LOT OF *DEAD BODIES* IN HER WAKE.

AND YET SHE DIDN'T KILL *YOU* WHEN SHE HAD THE CHANCE.

NO, SHE *FLED.*
JUST LIKE *GUILTY PEOPLE* DO.

I DON'T TRY TO EXPLAIN TO ROBERTS THAT THERE ARE A LOT OF REASONS A SPY MIGHT FLEE...

YOU STAY OUT LONG ENOUGH, YOU CAN FORGET WHO YOU'RE ***SUPPOSED*** TO TRUST.

BUT THE MAN DID HAVE ***ONE POINT***-- VELVET KNOWS HOW WE'LL RESPOND TO HER MOVES...

SO I DECIDE TO TRY A ***DIFFERENT TRAIL*** INSTEAD.

IF VELVET IS TRACING KELLER'S MOVEMENTS, THEN MAYBE I CAN FIND OUT ***WHY.***

I KNEW THAT SHE AND KELLER WERE CLOSER THAN HE ADMITTED IN HIS REPORTS.
HE ACTUALLY KNOCKED ME OUT ONCE FOR SLEEPING WITH HER.

SO IF ANYONE WAS GOING TO KNOW WHAT HE'D GOTTEN INTO...
...IT WOULD BE GRETCHEN.

THE PROBLEM IS, WHEN I GET THERE...
SHE'S ALREADY DEAD.

AND HER KILLERS ARE WAITING FOR ME.

I TAKE THE LONG WAY TO THE *SAFE HOUSE* AFTER THAT...

...BUT MY GUT WON'T LET ME GO IN.

ROBERTS

I should've never left the S.A.S.

...such as our Science Specialist.

OR ARE WE RUNNING A FUCKING **STEALTH SUIT** RENTAL, AND NO ONE TOLD ME?

IT'S NOT-- I JUST--I WAS **FRIENDS** WITH HER.

SHE...SHE **LIKED** TO SEE MY WORK. SO I ALLOWED HER ACCESS TO THE **LAB...**

SHE WAS THE DIRECTOR'S **SECRETARY...**I COULDN'T HAVE **KNOWN...**

...I COULDN'T HAVE...

CHRIST.

*Why were the **geniuses** always the biggest **idiots** when it came to women?*

If it had been up to me, he'd be rotting in a cell...
But no, the men at the top say the agency needs his brain.

So my only consolation is our little "Joe 90" working harder than ever to prove his loyalty.
Finding leads the Rude Boys and I can run down.

Getting me out of the murk, back to where I can at least tell myself I know where the ground is.

It was him who found her accomplice...her way out...Burke. Known smuggler and mercenary.
Our files have him listed as out-of-business.
CONFIDENTIAL
Serial
ISSUED BY THE
OFFICE OF
Burke c1958

But as Velvet's proving, no one ever really retires in this world.
That would be too simple.

But I've got simple well in hand now.
I find this Burke, and he tells me where she is.

GOD DAMN IT ALL...
So what's bugging me?
I can't stop thinking about what Colt said. That maybe there's something else going on.

Christ, I'm starting to become like them. Looking for every possible side of an answer...
SERGEANT ROBERTS? IT'S THE LONDON OFFICE...
THIS IS ROBERTS.
WHERE? AMSTERDAM?
AND WHERE WAS HER LAYOVER?
OH, FUCK ME...
SHE'S IN LONDON.
And just like that, it gets simple again.

The bitch lured me away, then swapped passports with some moron...
OUT OF THE WAY!

Even using an old agency legend, that she had to know we'd catch.

She's come home and she doesn't care if we know.

MOVE!

I NEED TO SEE THE DIRECTOR-- NOW!
I'M AFRAID HE'S NOT IN YET, SIR.

WHAT DO YOU *MEAN* HE'S NOT IN? IT'S HALF-PAST *LUNCH!*
I'M AFRAID IT'S WORSE THAN THAT, SERGEANT...

...*THIS* WAS JUST LEFT BY A MESSENGER, FOR *YOU*.

I TOOK THE *LIBERTY* OF OPENING IT...

CHRIST...

THAT'S *THIS MORNING'S* PAPER?
Daily Mail
BUDGET SPECIAL
First the good news: Bigger pensions and subsidies
for bread, milk and butter. Now the bad: Up go
Life for the 'gentle' nurse who murdered
IT *IS.*
IS THERE A NOTE? WHAT DOES SHE *WANT?*
NO *NOTE,* NO.
WHERE IS THIS? DO YOU-- IT LOOKS *FAMILIAR--*
THAT... THAT'S THE *SECRETARIAL LEVEL*...IN THE CAR PARK...
...UNDER THE BUILDING.
OH...OH, CHRIST...

ALLIED

LONDON – ARC-7 HQ
Fucking Christ, they are badly unprepared...
Twenty-two minutes from **time of delivery** until they **begin** evacuating.

They're lucky I'm not **actually** planning to blow the place up.

Okay, all clear... or good enough...

So then...let's try this **again**...

Spent a few days practicing the suit's glide function when I was on the run...
Hopefully I'm just as good without the river to break my fall.
And hopefully Mrs. Hodgkins is still pretending she's quit smoking...
ELEVENTH FLOOR...TENTH...
...as if none of us notice her blowing it out the window.
YES!
Thank god for bad habits.

Which should be **more** than--

STOP!

STOP **RIGHT THERE,** MISS TEMPLETON...

DO **NOT** GIVE ME A REASON TO **SHOOT** YOU.

PART THREE

SIX HOURS EARLIER
OUT.

TEMPLETON... WHAT ARE YOU *DOING?*

WHAT I *HAVE* TO. COME ON...*UP.*
AND DON'T EVEN *THINK* ABOUT HITTING ME WITH THAT CANE.
PECKS GARAGE

THEY'LL BE *LOOKING* FOR ME *ALREADY,* YOU KNOW...
MY *MEN* WILL HAVE BEEN--
NO. YOUR MEN ARE IN *HOSPITAL* IN SOUTH LONDON, WITH *NO IDENTIFICATION...*

...AND SO *DOPED UP* THEY WON'T WAKE UNTIL AT LEAST TOMORROW.

YOU FORGET I USED TO BE GOOD AT THIS, DIRECTOR.

GARAGE
NOW PLEASE, SIR, TAKE A SEAT...
WE HAVE SOME WORK TO DO.

WHAT--?

YOU'RE MAKING A BOMB?
VELVET... YOU CAN'T BE--

SIT.

I'VE SPENT WEEKS DEFENDING YOU...
SAYING THERE MUST BE EXTENUATING CIRCUMSTANCES...
THAT YOU CAN'T HAVE BEEN TURNED...
PECKS GARAGE

AND YOU-- YOU WANT TO STRAP A BOMB TO ME--
--LIKE SOME DAMN TERRORIST?

IT'S NOT LIKE THAT.

THEN TELL ME WHAT IT IS LIKE.
BECAUSE IT LOOKS LIKE SIMONSON IS RIGHT ABOUT YOU...

...AND I'D RATHER NOT BELIEVE I COULD BE THAT WRONG TWICE IN MY LIFE.
THAT'S JUST IT, ISN'T IT?
YOU PEOPLE GET IT WRONG, AND WE PAY THE PENALTY.

VELVET... WHAT IS THIS ABOUT?

I REALLY DO WISH I COULD TELL YOU...
BECAUSE IT'S NOT YOU I DON'T TRUST.

YOU KNOW WHAT YOU SOUND LIKE?
LIKE EVERY OPERATIVE WHO EVER GOT LOST DOWN THEIR OWN RABBIT HOLE.

OH, BELIEVE ME, I KNOW...

NOW GET ON THE GODDAMNED STOOL.

And I know what time the **secretarial level** fills up...

So I know when it'll be **deserted**, for the next part of my plan.

THAT'S IT... NOW DON'T MOVE...

UHHNN--
I KNOW WHAT YOU'RE THINKING, AND IT'S ***NOT*** GOING TO WORK.
YOU ***DON'T,*** ACTUALLY.

WHEN THE BUILDING'S IN ***LOCKDOWN,*** THE VAULTS ***WON'T*** OPEN.
BLOODY ***ELEVATORS*** WON'T EVEN WORK.
THANKS FOR THE CONCERN...

...BUT I ***KNOW*** ALL THAT.
NOW I'M GOING TO HAVE TO ***HANDCUFF*** YOU AGAIN, SIR.

Stealing another car and driving back out is a snap.
I'm just some **secretary** taking an early lunch.

Then it's just technical details and waiting...

I'm on the roof across the way **long before** my messenger delivers the **photos.**
I start counting in my head the **second** the evacuation begins...

....and I leap when I'm **sure** they're in the garage.
FLANK LEFT... CHECK **ALL** THESE VEHICLES...
SHE COULD BE ***ANYWHERE.***

It's a bit much, I admit...
...but there are few distractions more effective than an Agency Director sitting on a ticking time bomb.

And maybe that's what tips off Sgt. Roberts... that it's too much.
DAMN IT... THIS IS JUST WHAT SHE WANTS...

Or maybe it's the Director's expression.
The fact that he's not afraid.

ROBERTS!?
IT'S A BLOODY TRICK!

SHE'S IN THE BUILDING!
It doesn't really matter what does it...

...the important thing is he's **early.**
This asshole's screwing up my time frame.
I AM NOT FUCKING AROUND!
ON YOUR KNEES-- HANDS BEHIND YOUR HEAD--
NOW!
Which means... he just ran up twelve flights of stairs.
He's winded... it shows...
I WON'T SAY IT AGAIN--
Let's hope it slows him down.

SHIT!
--UHHN--!
STAY DOWN!
DO NOT FUCKING MOVE!
...FUHH...

Stealth suit really is bulletproof...
...good to know...
FFF--!
...THAT FUCKING... HURT...
YOU STUPID... BASTARD...

...so he wants his **gun** back.

Predictable.

NN--

AAAHHHH--!

...AH... JESUS... FUCK...
OH, QUIT YOUR BLOODY WHINING...

TRY GETTING SHOT IN THE RIBS SOMETIME...

It takes three cracks to the head to knock him out.
Stupid thick-skulled bastard.

...UUHH...

...WHH... FUHH...
DIRECTOR MANNING

There's an empty spot on the Director's wall where a picture of the two of US used to hang.

I knew it wouldn't be there...but still...

...that actually hurts more than my cracked ribs.

YES, THIS IS ARC-7, DIRECTORATE ALPHA... ECHO ECHO NINE...
CAN YOU CONNECT ME WITH THE SUPERVISOR?

OF COURSE, MA'AM...
THANK YOU.

WELL...THIS IS GETTING TO BE A *HABIT.*

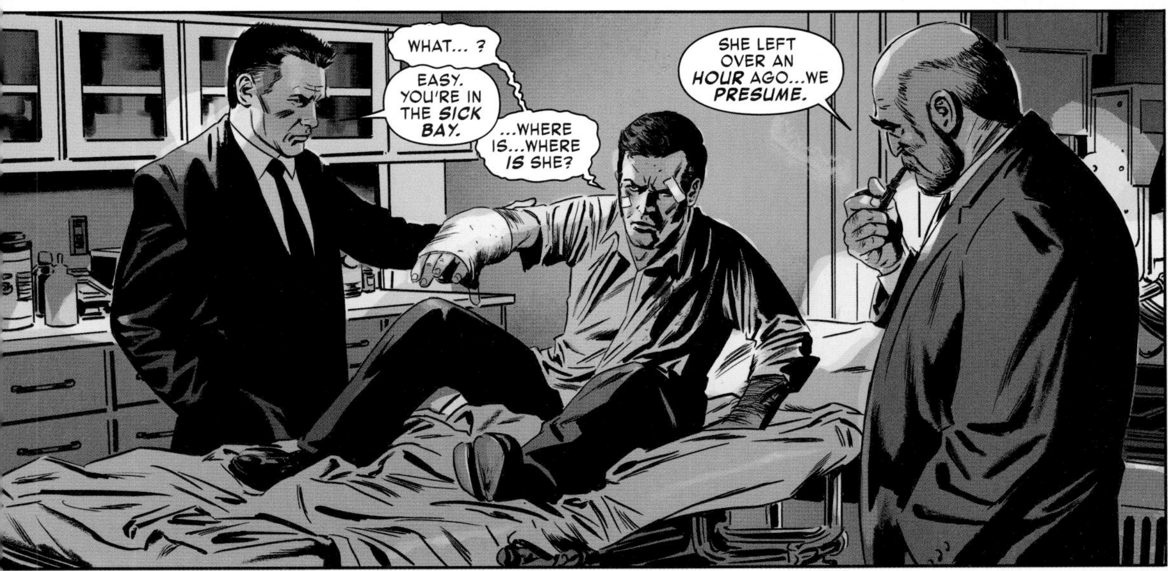
WHAT... ?
EASY. YOU'RE IN THE *SICK BAY.*
...WHERE IS...WHERE *IS* SHE?
SHE LEFT OVER AN *HOUR* AGO...WE *PRESUME.*

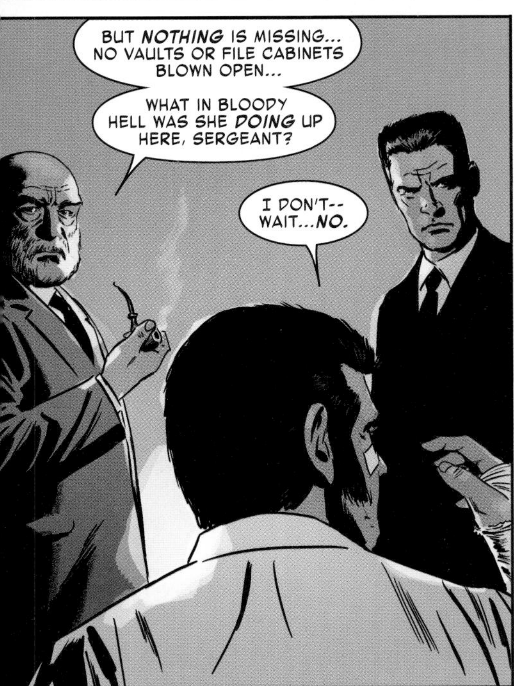
BUT *NOTHING* IS MISSING... NO VAULTS OR FILE CABINETS BLOWN OPEN...
WHAT IN BLOODY HELL WAS SHE *DOING* UP HERE, SERGEANT?
I DON'T-- WAIT...*NO.*

RIGHT BEFORE I PASSED OUT, I *HEARD* HER...
SHE WAS IN *YOUR* OFFICE...

...ON THE *TELEPHONE.*

TEN MILES NORTH OF LONDON

MITCH SAYS HE'S TO BE TRANSFERRED TO *LONDON* FOR QUESTIONING, AND I JUST FUCKIN' DO AS I'M *TOLD*, DON'T I?

BUT, LIKE, YOU *KNOW*... RIGHT?

YOU KNOW WHO THIS *IS?*

I JUST BLOODY *SAID*...

RAN SOME SPECIAL INTEL UNIT... BEFORE HE LOST HIS MIND.
RIGHT...THINK I HEARD SOME'A THE OTHER GUARDS TALK ABOUT HIM.

YEAH... LOTTA RUMORS ABOUT THIS ONE...

WILLIAMSON SAYS HE WAS A MOLE FOR THE SOVIETS...

BUT MITCH SAYS HE WAS THE SOLE SURVIVOR WHEN HIS UNIT GOT WIPED OUT...

WELL, WHATEVER HE USED TO BE...
ALL I SEE HERE IS YET ANOTHER CATATONIC, DRUGGED-OUT OLD BASTARD.
GOOD BLOODY LUCK TO WHOEVER'S TRYIN' TO GET INFORMATION OUT OF THIS ONE.
HOPE THEY LIKE HEARING THEMSELF TALK...

"THE ATTACK HAPPENED TWO MILES OUT FROM THE FACILITY.
"SHE TOOK OUT THE LEFT FRONT TIRE AS THEY WERE *TURNING...*
"...THEN LET *GRAVITY* DO THE REAL WORK FOR HER."

SHE PICKED THE SPOT PERFECTLY...
TUMBLED THEM RIGHT INTO THE TRENCH...
AMBULANCE
STOP
RHE 52
"A SOFT LANDING... JUST UPSIDE DOWN."
AMBULANCE
ONE OF THE GUARDS WAS OUT COLD WHEN WE GOT HERE.
THE OTHER DOESN'T REMEMBER *ANYTHING* BUT THE CRASH...
"BUT CLEARLY SHE DRAGGED THE *PRISONER* FROM THE VAN TO A CAR SHE'D LEFT HERE EARLIER..."

...SO SHE DOESN'T TRUST HIM ENOUGH TO WANT HIM ON THE BACK OF HER MOTORCYCLE.
NO...SHE WOULDN'T.

SO, WHO'S THIS PRISONER?

WE CAN'T TALK ABOUT THAT HERE.
SCREW *PROTOCOL,* LIEUTENANT.

THAT BITCH BROKE INTO OUR HQ FOR THE *SOLE PURPOSE* OF ARRANGING THIS MAN'S *ESCAPE...*
SO I NEED TO KNOW WHO HE IS RIGHT BLOODY *NOW.*

OR DO YOU NOT *WANT ME* TO CATCH HER?

PART FOUR

The problem was, I needed someone from the early days of the agency...
Someone I was sure wasn't the one setting me up.
And Damian Lake fit that bill perfectly, since he'd spent the last fourteen years in a high security insane asylum.
But back in 1956, before my entire life went flying off the rails...
...Damian was the head of our Intel division.

I didn't know him well then, and he'd been transferred to Paris Station before I became the Director's Girl Friday...

But the official story of how he'd ended up in a padded cell had always felt... well, a bit too "official."

After his move to Paris, a code station he was overseeing had been hit by the KGB...

...and Damian was the only survivor.
They found him surrounded by the dead, muttering to himself like a lunatic.

It wasn't the first time a sharp mind had snapped in the face of horror...Christ, I knew that well.

But still, it felt like a cover-up.
Victim sounds much better in a report to the Prime Minister than traitor does, after all...

But now? Now I didn't know what to think.
...WHH... HNH...

WELL...I KNEW THEY'D GET AROUND TO ME AGAIN EVENTUALLY...

BUT I DIDN'T THINK YOU'D BE THE ONE THEY SENT...
OR I'D HAVE BEEN LOOKING FORWARD TO IT.

I'M AFRAID YOU'VE GOT IT WRONG...I'M JUST HERE TO TALK.
WHATEVER HAPPENS *BEYOND THAT* IS UP TO YOU.

IS IT, NOW?

YES. IT DEPENDS ON WHAT YOU SAY.

REALLY? MANNING CAN'T GET ANYTHING OUT OF ME...
BUT HE THINKS I'LL FALL FOR A *HONEY TRAP?*

I'M NOT SURE IF THAT'S A COMPLIMENT OR AN INSULT.

NEITHER AM *I.*
CAN I HAVE ONE OF THOSE?

NO.
CIGARETTES ARE FOR BOYS WHO *COOPERATE.*

WELL THEN... WHAT DID YOU WANT TO TALK ABOUT?
MY HUSBAND... *CODENAME MOCKINGBIRD.*

HNNH...
SO YOU *FINALLY* FIGURED OUT HE WASN'T A TRAITOR.

WHAT DID THEY DO TO TIP YOU OFF?
KILLED ANOTHER *AGENT* AND FRAMED ME FOR IT.

AH...THAT OLD CLASSIC.

SO, YOU KNEW ALL ALONG? THAT HE WAS INNOCENT?
NO. I THOUGHT OUR RUSSIAN INTEL WAS GOOD OR I WOULDN'T HAVE PASSED IT ALONG.

I DIDN'T LIKE IT, BUT AGENTS TURN... IT HAPPENS.

"THEN A REPORT LANDED ON MY DESK IN PARIS THREE YEARS AFTER...
"ONE OF OUR ASSETS IN AFRICA, MENTIONING SOME COMPANY BUYING UP LAND AFTER WE'D JUST REMOVED A LOCAL WARLORD."

AND THAT SOUNDED FAMILIAR, BUT I DIDN'T KNOW WHY.

"SO I LOOKED INTO THIS COMPANY--NOMEX INTERNATIONAL, THEY WERE CALLED...
"...AFTER A FEW DAYS IN THE RECORDS ROOM, I FOUND OUT THEY WERE A DIVISION OF ANOTHER COMPANY, TITANIC HOLDINGS."

AND THAT'S WHEN I REMEMBERED THE THING THAT HAD BEEN NAGGING AT ME...
WHICH WAS WHAT?

MOCKINGBIRD HAD MENTIONED TITANIC, WITH THE SAME OBSERVATION...
THEM MOVING INTO PLACES WHERE WE, OR THE C.I.A., HAD JUST BURNED-OUT SOME VILLAGE...
...OR BLOWN UP AN ENTIRE ECONOMY.

"SO I PUT ONE OF MY TEAMS ON IT... I WANTED TO KNOW EVERYTHING ABOUT THEM.
"BUT INTEL WAS SURPRISINGLY HARD TO COME BY FOR AN INTERNATIONAL CONGLOMERATE.

"STILL, ONE OF MY MEN TRACKED DOWN A LOG OF THEIR FIRST BOARD MEETING...
"AND THERE WAS A NAME ON IT THAT GAVE ME THAT SAME PIT OF MY STOMACH FEELING THE NOMEX REPORT HAD DONE."

"EXCEPT WHEN I WENT TO LOOK IT UP IN *THE VAULT*, ALL RECORD OF THAT *LEGEND* WAS GONE...SCRUBBED.

"LIKE OUR *PIERRE* HAD NEVER EXISTED...

"THAT'S WHEN I KNEW I'D MADE A MISTAKE."

THE SAME ONE YOUR HUSBAND, AND NOW I SUPPOSE *YOU*...ALSO MADE.

"I TRIED TO SHUT DOWN MY TEAM, MAKE THE ENTIRE *INVESTIGATION* GO AWAY...

"BUT I WAS TOO LATE. THEY WERE ALREADY DEAD."

I MANAGED TO MAKE IT AS FAR AS THE *TRAIN STATION* BEFORE THEY CAUGHT ME...

THE REST, YOU KNOW...

BECAUSE ARC-7 MAY HAVE WIPED "PIERRE DUPREY" FROM THEIR RECORDS...
BUT THE D.S.T. HAD *PHOTOS* FOR EVERY VICHY OFFICER DURING THE NAZI OCCUPATION.

I HAVE HIS *PICTURE.*

THAT WOULD SEEM LIKE A *PERFECT REASON* TO KILL YOU.
EXCEPT IF I *DIE,* HIS PHOTO AND THE WHOLE FILE...THEY GO PUBLIC.

I'M THE EX-HEAD OF INTEL, *REMEMBER?* I KNOW THIS GAME.

SO THEN...WHO IS IT? WHO'S *PIERRE?*
NUH UH... THAT'S *NOT* HOW IT'S PLAYED.

I'LL HAVE ONE OF THOSE *CIGARETTES* NOW...

...AND THEN WE CAN TALK ABOUT HOW WE GET TO *PARIS.*

How we get to Paris is this: the long way.
We drive north into Scotland and bribe our way onto a freighter out of Inverness.
We dock in Copenhagen, where we mingle among the crowd at the airport...
And I "find" us some new passports.
A few hops later--Copenhagen to Luxembourg to Geneva--and it's the next night...
And we're on a train winding through the Alps.
Like I said, the long way.

And the whole time, I watch Damian out of the corner of my eye, not sure if I believe him...
...but unable to deny that his story makes sense.
Or, as much sense as what's happened to me, at least.

YOU'RE LOOKING AT THE SKY LIKE YOU THOUGHT YOU'D NEVER SEE IT AGAIN.
--WHAT...?

OH...I WAS ACTUALLY JUST... SPACED OUT.
THE PILLS THOSE BASTARDS HAD ME ON...

I'M STILL FEELING...
...NOT LIKE MYSELF.

YOU WILL SOON.
THE PAST MONTH IS THE FIRST TIME I'VE FELT LIKE MYSELF SINCE... SINCE...

SINCE BEFORE YOU WERE MARRIED?
YES...THAT'S WHAT I WAS THINKING.

YES, WELL...I SUPPOSE IN *THEIR* VIEW, THEY WERE SIMPLY BEING EXPEDIENT.

I MEAN, WE'RE ALL PAWNS ANYWAY...
WHAT DOES IT *MATTER* TO THEM IF WE DON'T KNOW *WHICH* GAME WE'RE *PLAYING?*

STILL, THAT WAS A CRUEL THING TO DO.

CHRIST, HAVE I *MISSED* LIQUOR.
SO YOU KEEP SAYING...

ARE YOU DRUNK ENOUGH YET TO TELL ME WHO PIERRE IS?
NOT EVEN CLOSE.

I SHOULD PUNCH YOU.
I CAN HIT REALLY HARD.

COME ON, TEMPLETON. I CAN'T GIVE UP MY ONLY PIECE.

EVEN IF YOU'RE AS ON THE LEVEL AS YOU SEEM, THE SECOND I TELL YOU ANYTHING...
I'M JUST AN OLD MAN SLOWING DOWN YOUR HUNT.

BE LUCKY IF YOU DIDN'T TOSS ME OFF THE TRAIN.

I'M CONSIDERING IT ANYWAY.

AND HERE I WAS HOPING YOU WERE GOING TO TRY *SEDUCING* IT OUT OF ME.

WOULD THAT WORK?

IT'S BEEN AN AWFULLY LONG TIME, BUT *PROBABLY* NOT.
YOU'RE WELCOME TO TRY, THOUGH.

I'LL *PASS.* PROBABLY CAN'T GET IT UP, ANYWAY, ALL THOSE *PILLS* THEY HAD YOU ON.
OH, COME ON NOW. *THAT'S* OVER THE LINE.

BUT SPEAKING OF MY JOHN THOMAS, I NEED TO VISIT THE *LOO.*
WE JUST CROSSED INTO FRANCE...WE'LL BE CHANGING TRAINS SOON.

"SO, I'VE READ THE AUTHORIZED VERSION..."

...BUT I'M GUESSING THERE'S MORE TO THIS FINAL REPORT?
THE ONE WHERE HIS TEAM ALL DIE YET HE MIRACULOUSLY ESCAPES WITHOUT A SCRATCH?
OH YES, THERE'S MUCH MORE.

"THERE ALWAYS WAS WITH DAMIAN."

I SAW IT, THAT SOMETHING WAS JUST...NOT RIGHT WITH HIM.
BUT YOU COULDN'T SAY ANYTHING...

"...THE MAN WAS A BLOODY WAR HERO."

HE RAN SPIES IN FRANCE, POLAND... EVEN **BERLIN**, NEAR THE END.

NO ONE WANTED TO **HEAR** HE MIGHT BE LOSING HIS MIND.

SO **HE** KILLED THEM, THEN?

YES. SEVEN OF OUR PEOPLE.

WHICH WAS **NOT** THE *"I TOLD YOU SO"* MOMENT I'D BEEN HOPING FOR.

...PLEASE KEEP YOUR HANDS WHERE WE CAN SEE THEM.

YOU'RE UNDER ARREST.

This is why you don't work alone in this world...
Not for as long as I've been, at least.
Because you don't realize it...but you get lonely when no one else is on your side.
I SAID YOU ARE BEING ARRESTED.
DO YOU SPEAK FRENCH? DO YOU UNDERSTAND?
You want someone to see what you're seeing...what you're up against.
YES...I UNDERSTAND...
So you grasp at straws...
AHKK--!

You look at someone else who's been accused... who's been isolated...
GYAA--!
STOP!
And you see a potential ally...
BLAM BLAM BLAM BLAM BLAM BLAM
...when you should know to be much smarter than that.

This is very bad.
Damian Lake isn't just putting up a roadblock to cover his escape...
The Gendarme just opened fire on me in public.
The bastard's blown my cover.
They know who I am...
Or at least who Interpol is saying I am.
FUCK.

He wasn't lying. He does know how to play this game...
Because he's left me only one move...
...and it sidelines me.

PART FIVE

Christ--they're **already** on me **again?**

Have I gotten **that** slow?

He wants me setting off every alarm ARC-7 has set...

...while he just waltzes back into Paris to collect his evidence.

Assuming there was any truth in the story he told...which is a big assumption.

But I was taught the best lies are the ones that hew closest to the truth.
He's probably already on the next train...

Or he's switching to a rental car at the station...
KFF--!

And once he's got what he's after in Paris...

...he'll be gone.
GUHTT--!

I need to--
FUCK.

FUCK!
Don't kill the dog-- don't kill the dog --
Don't kill the--OW! Motherfucker!
Teeth can't **puncture** the stealth suit--
--but I feel them all the way to my **bones.**
Come on, fucker... choke out...
Son of a bitch... arm feels nearly broken, **sprained** for sure...
Maybe I **should've** killed it...

No...I can't be mad at the poor thing for doing what it's been trained to.

But I **am** mad now.

No denying that.

I WAS TRYING TO BE *NICE*...

BUT YOU ASSHOLES MADE ME HURT A *DOG*...

Still. Have to make it quick.
There'll be more of them.
These men didn't appear by magic, a truck dropped them off...
And it'll be **back around** soon.
I spotted a farm house from the train, about a mile south...
Let's hope they have something I can **drive** besides a tractor...

I move slow and stay hidden...
While my mind races ahead, trying to figure out where I'll **find** Damian, if I can get to Paris.
I've been looking for a **double-agent,** but his "Pierre Duprey" story implies something else...
A **different** kind of corruption.
But without Damian all I have is that... a **story...**
Told by a **traitor.**

Yet still, the **details** of it nag at me...

Because they fit too well.

Trying to **out-guess** someone that I **know** is playing me.

Just get the **car**, Velvet... get moving.

Just--

SHIT.

THAT'S ENOUGH...NOW **RESTRAIN** HER.

Dizzy...ears ringing...still I **recognize** him...

Jean Bellanger... ARC-7's Paris Station Chief...

One of the men on my **list...**

Christ...Damian must've betrayed me hours ago...

Gave them time to set a trap...

And the goddamned Gendarme pushed me right into it...

HELLO, TEMPLETON... NICE TO SEE YOU STILL FOLLOW SOME OF YOUR TRAINING.

YOU KNOW, I ALWAYS HAD A BAD FEELING ABOUT YOU... YOU BROKE TOO EASILY, I THOUGHT.

MANNING JUST HAD A BLIND SPOT WHERE YOU WERE CONCERNED...

...TELL ME WHERE TO FIND DAMIAN LAKE.
...OH... NOW I GET IT...
THE BASTARD WASN'T ENTIRELY FULL OF SHIT...

HE REALLY DOES HAVE SOMETHING... DOESN'T HE...?
IS IT ON YOU... IS THAT WHY HE WANTED TO GO TO PARIS...?

I DON'T KNOW WHAT YOU'RE TALKING ABOUT...
But I can see it in his eyes...fear.

I say the name, just to make sure...
PIERRE DUPREY.

And I see it again...
SHUT THIS BITCH UP.

...for just a

There's a moment just at the edge of consciousness...
...where you find a different point of view...
...where you can circle your problems...almost endlessly...
...until your eyes finally open.
That's when a **new thought** hits me... about Damian Lake...
...WHAT...
And when I realize the car I'm in the back of **isn't** moving...
I know I'm right.

Damian didn't go to Paris...
...OH, THAT FUCKER...
He was using me as **bait**.
I didn't walk into the trap... Bellanger did.

I spent the last fifteen years playing **secretary...** living a lie...
VELVET

...but he spent those years **planning.**

WELCOME TO THE REAL GAME.
SEE YOU SOON
-D

SHIT...

All these weeks on the run, I've just been angry...

Self-righteous.

And it's so stupid...I know...

But I'd actually forgotten to be afraid.

EPILOGUE

LONDON--TEN DAYS LATER

THANK YOU FOR *MEETING ME*, SIR...
WITH ASSISTANT DIRECTOR SIMONSON IN *PARIS*, I DIDN'T KNOW WHO ELSE TO GO TO...
IS THERE SOME NEWS, ON *EITHER* OF THEM?

OH, *NO...* NO SIR, STILL NO SIGHTINGS.
THIS IS ABOUT SOMETHING *ELSE.*

AND I ASSUME THERE'S A REASON WE COULDN'T DO THIS DURING OFFICE HOURS?

I'M NOT SURE... MAYBE...
JUST SPIT IT OUT, SERGEANT.

I'VE BEEN LISTENING TO THE TAPES FROM DAMIAN LAKE'S INITIAL INTERROGATION...
AND I MISSED IT AT FIRST, BUT THERE'S THIS ONE THING HE SAYS...

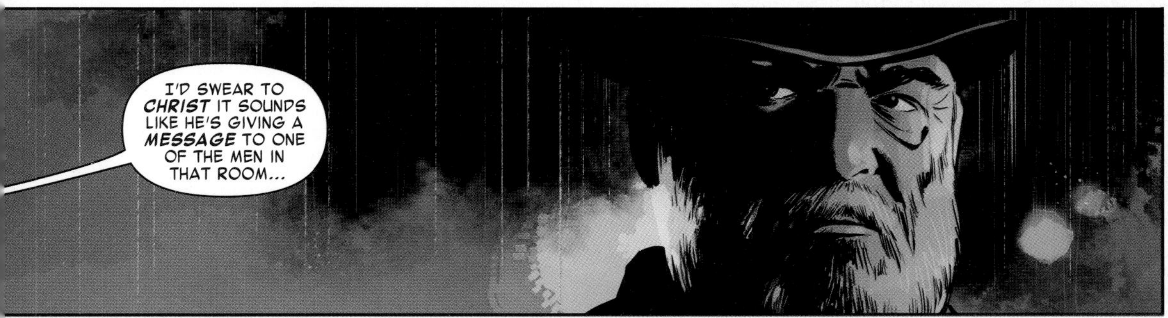
I'D SWEAR TO CHRIST IT SOUNDS LIKE HE'S GIVING A MESSAGE TO ONE OF THE MEN IN THAT ROOM...

LIKE HE'S REACHING OUT TO ANOTHER TRAITOR.

I WAS IN THAT ROOM.

YES...YOU, BELLANGER, AND HILLERMAN...
WITH SIMONSON IN THE MONITORING BOOTH.

THAT'S--
??

GKK...

...NNHH...

SORRY, OLD MAN...

...SOME THINGS SIMPLY *HAVE* TO BE *DONE.*

IT'S NOTHING PERSONAL.

TO BE CONTINUED